(Manic Street Prea

7 AM, February 1 1995. The Embassy Hotel, Bayswater Road, London. Oblivious to the season's biting early-morning wind and steel grey skies, a gaunt, shaven headed man steps from the pavement of the hotel's entrance, climbs into his modest silver Vauxhall Cavalier, and speeds off, heading west. It is Richey James Edward, charismatic singer with The Manic Street Preachers, and he is never to be seen again.

Due to fly out that afternoon from Heathrow Airport with the rest of the band for a US tour to promote their most recent album, he quite literally vanishes into thin air.

Since their emergence in the summer of 1989 no-one was in any serious doubt that the Manics had something special. Their only problem was overcoming the current trend of dance music, the funky, groove tinged rock from Madchester, and concurrent fashion for baggy, oversized jeans. The Manic Street Preachers seemed to have a better chance of running for Parliament than cracking into the dance market.

Some thought they'd be a flash in the pan, that their brand of punky-glam rock and New York Dolls imagery would fail miserably, a painful embarrassment for the band. After all, the leaning towards dance music was in many ways a reaction to the Guns'N Roses and Bon Jovi overkill that music fans of a more thoughtful disposition had had to endure during the mid-Eighties.

While The Stone Roses and Primal Scream somehow managed to drop their rock aesthetics and slip under the net, most others failed to impress the ecstasy-fuelled love crowd. It would be another four years before guitar-based bands reclaimed top dog status under the guise of Britpop.

The Manic Street Preachers were one, if not the only, English metal/punk band to ride, thrive in and conquer not only the dance scene. How did they do this, with such odds stacked against them? And what led Richey Edward's to disappear just as the Manics were reaching stardom? How have the remaining members coped with his absence? Is he dead or just hiding? Some of these questions are easy to answer but others, his disappearance, lie buried. Only time will reveal the truth of what has, or hasn't, happened to him.

METROPOLITAN POLICE SERVICE

Form 584 (C)   Station Copy

PNC W/M No:

Please use BLOCK CAPITALS / Do NOT fold
*Delete as appropriate

Stn. Ref. No: **584/21**

Class class: (~~person missing~~) person, body found /
absentee from care / mental absconder / hosper

Send photograph if available to B14 with Form 584. Original will be returned after copying

*LIMITED / ENQUIRY   Station: HARROW ROAD

Surname:	Forenames:	(Male) Female Unknown	DOB (If not known give age)
EDWARDS	RICHARD		22 12 67

Ethnic appearance: (White European) / Dark European / Negroid / Asian / Oriental / Arab / Doubt   Height: 5 ft 8 ins

Alias: —

Marks, scars, tattoos, physical peculiarities:
SEVERAL TATTOOS
ROSE 'USELESS GENERATION'
ON LEFT ARM.

Birthplace: BLACKWOOD

Nationality: WELSH

Warning signals: (drugs, suicidal, depressed, violent, etc.)
ON ANTI DEPRESSANTS.

Habits / other characteristics:
(smokes, drinks, etc.)
SMOKES

Date of incident: 12 95 0700	Date of report: 22 95

Cross Ref., other person(s) involved:

Build: (slim) / medium / heavy / other

Hair: colour SHAVED / SHAVED   length   style

*Beard / moustache / wig / other:

Eyes: colour BROWN   *glasses / contact lenses

Complexion: PALE

Clothing—include full description and colour:

Jumper   N/K.

Trousers

Skirt

Topcoat

Jacket: Further tattoos - 2 ornate tattoos
Shirt   on shoulders (colourful but details N/K).
Footwear
Other

Jewellery:

Address from which missing: LONDON EMBASSY HOTEL

Home address if different: 6 ANSON CT, SCHOONER WAY, ATLANTIC WHARF, CARDIFF

Circumstances: Subject is a member of a band and was staying in London embassy hotel with another band member before flying to USA on business. Subject was seen by hotel staff leaving hotel on 12 95 at 0700 + has not been seen since. His passport is missing but all his belongings are still in his hotel room. Subject has made a previous suicide attempt + is taking anti-depressants.

Date / time last seen: 12 95 0700

School or Occupation: MEMBER OF POP BAND

Mental absconders: Order under S   MHA 19   NOT to be arrested after:

Care Order: To   Social Services
             at

INFORMANT Name
Address 8 P
UXBRIDGE
Publicity authorised:

ACTION REFER

Checks: PNC
MSS: To: B14/86(4) S
Transferred to:

Supervising

CANCELLATION B14
Supervising O

M.P.91

"A lot of people had terrible childhood's but personally, up to the age of 13, I was ecstatically happy. People treated me very well, my dog was beautiful, I lived with my nan and she was beautiful. School's nothing, you go there, come back and just play football in the fields. Then I moved from my nan's and started comprehensive school and everything started to go wrong." *Richey: October 1994*

The Manic Street Preachers story begins in the small, now largely benumbed mining town of Blackwood in South Wales where James Dean Bradfield, his cousin Sean Moore, Nicky Wire (nee Jones) and Richey 'Edwards' (or 'James' as he preferred) all came of age. They lived within a mile of each other, and attended the same infants, junior and comprehensive schools. The days at Oakdale Comprehensive and the nights in Blackwood were bleak and unvarying, and the four boys knew little of the social lives that cities can offer.

"Comprehensive school was the most depressing time for all of us," recalled Richey. "They either write you off or fit you in. If you're not academically gifted, it's 'fuck you'. If you are, it's, 'The banks are coming next week for a talk, and we think you should go'."

Whatever their attitudes, there was no doubting their academic potential: all the future Manics achieved A-levels. Sean Moore's was in music; Bradfield and Wire picked up three each, but it was Edwards who really excelled, gaining three straight A's.

"Comprehensive school was the most depressing time for all of us."

RICHEY

After the exams cousins James and Sean decided they'd had enough of school. They'd already been living together for some years. After an unpleasant parental split Sean found himself on James' doorstep, and for the next 12 years they were brought up together, house-mates and even bunk-mates. Hiding away in their tiny room, they read voraciously, listened and dreamed of music every day and night for years. As for work, James collected the dole and practised guitar whilst Sean took a desk job with the Civil Service.

Meanwhile, encouraged by their exam results, Richey and Nicky opted for university. Richey was accepted at Cardiff University, Nick at Portsmouth Polytechnic, but they were soon reunited since Nicky opted out after three weeks and transferred to Cardiff. During the next couple of years they became inseparable friends, bonding over music, literature and drink. Nicky majored in Politics while Richey read Political History. At the same time they talked of forming a band. All four had remained in close contact, and when Richey and Nick learnt that James and Sean had been practising their instruments, the two students began piecing together lyrics. A combination of Karl Marx, Greil Marcus and punk percolated into their trademark riot-ranting political lyrics.

"We discovered The Sex Pistols and The Rolling Stones at the same time as we discovered literature..." NICKY

"The first time I ever saw Richey cutting himself was in University, revising for his finals..." JAMES

"That's where we've nicked all our lyrics from, really," says Nicky. "We discovered The Sex Pistols and The Rolling Stones at the same time as we discovered literature. They seemed the same thing to us – both really exciting."

Towards the end of their stay at university Nicky Wire began to notice traits of disturbing behaviour in his best friend. Obsessed with the glamorous, self-destructive behaviour and emaciated vanity of past and present rock stars, Richey began to drink heavily, eat very little and, strangest of all, cut, gouge and mutilate his arms on a regular basis. Sid Vicious aside, this had little to do with emulating the habits of rock stars. Something was definitely wrong with young Richey's psyche. Depression and an extreme form of vanity, now recognised as anorexia, was ravaging Richey. He was losing control. When Nicky, Sean and James questioned Richey on the subject, he claimed he was cutting himself as a kind of therapy to regain his self-control.

"I started drinking in my first term at university," Richey told *New Musical Express*. "It was something that I'd never allowed myself to do, but it was just a question of getting myself to sleep. It was so noisy, and I needed to get to sleep at a certain time and wake at a certain time, and drinking gave me that opportunity.

"When it came for me to do my finals, I suddenly realised that I can't go in to do my finals pissed. So the way for me to gain control was cutting myself a little bit. Only with a compass – you know, vague little cuts – and not eating very much. Then I found I was really good during the day. I slept, felt good about myself, I could do all my exams. I got a 2:1 so I wasn't a 100% success, but I got through it, I did it. I remember James came down to see me in the Easter holidays before I did my finals. I wasn't very healthy then. But I did alright on my exams."

James remembers witnessing the first time he saw Richey cut himself. "The first time I ever saw Richey cutting himself was in university, revising for his finals. And he just got a compass and went like that... (demonstrating across his arm)."

This perverse practice of self-mutilation would carry on throughout Richey's Manic career.

By the end of university, Richey's weight had dropped to below seven stone. Rarely venturing from his dorm, his drinking increased and he was evasive towards almost everyone. Being holed up in a tower block with hundreds of people with whom he had nothing in common, was, he said... " a really bad experience. I think if I'd been able to have a flat of my own, my memory would've been very different because I've never been good with very many people. I've always surrounded myself with just a few people."

While Richey and Nicky edged towards graduation in Cardiff, James and his cousin Sean reflected on what Gwent had to offer. Unhappy at the thought of desk jobs in the backwoods of Wales, they were desperate for their lives to change. A master-plan was needed to rescue them from the drabness of poverty, Wales and the only life they had known.

Still living together, James and Sean spent all their free time practising their musical instruments. James played guitar and listened to heavy punk rock, Sean played drums and listened to jazz. Gorging themselves on the latest bands, they would travel hundreds of miles and sleep rough under rail-tunnels to get to gigs. Videos, records and tapes littered the floor and posters and cut-outs of musicians covered the wall of their small room. The soundtrack to their lives was the blaring onslaught of music from their ever increasing record collection: Gang Of Four, Wire, the Pistols and Big Flame and The Clash featured heavily on the stereo. They became heavily smitten with the current excess-fuelled American metal bands, especially Guns'N Roses.

At the end of 1989 both Richey and Nicky graduated from
Cardiff University and returned home. Reunited with James and Sean,
the four quickly transformed their bedroom into a sort of hospice-
saloon-cum-practise room. Nicky, who had taken some basic guitar
lessons at school, soon joined Sean and James in bashing out their
favourite tunes of the moment; James on guitar, Sean on drums
and Nicky on rudimentary bass. Richey sat in the corner, perpetually
scribbling and drawing in notebooks, reading obscure political
literature and nursing vodka and lagers. The four never strayed far
from each other, and there was a special bond between Richey
and Nicky. They became inseparable, they dressed alike and adopted
the same hair styles.

As the musical proficiency of Sean, James and Nicky
developed, their tastes and attitudes towards rock and pop became
more varied and sophisticated. The British music scene in the late
Eighties, wherein individuality was suppressed by grey-suited
record company executives in favour of formula bands, no longer
impressed them. Bored with the drab synth-bands, they were of
a generation that sought upheaval and they braced themselves for
change – waiting, watching, hoping.

This was the era that just preceded the emergence of
The Stone Roses, The Happy Mondays and the house music explosion.
Opportunity abounded; record companies were eager to sign
anyone from techno bedroom boffins to 14-piece acid jazz combos.
If there ever was an ideal time to start a band this was it.

At the Manic's HQ in Wales, James, Sean, Nicky and
Richey pondered the over the current events in the weekly *NME*.
Then, probably over a few beers, it dawned on them. A way they could
join in the fun, get paid for doing it and, most importantly, escape.
It was so easy, form a band.

(TWO)

Towards the end of 1989 a backlash against the ecstasy-upped attitudes that had prevailed for the last few years was imminent. Young people had grown sick of the good-will sheen that masked the continuing problems of unemployment, poverty and an unsympathetic government. While the drugs had taken hold, the anger had evaporated. After the heads had cleared there was the realisation that they had been conned into ignorant bliss, and frustration followed, then anger. The time was right for an explosion.

Initially trading under the name Betty Blue, the band that became The Manic Street Preachers comprised James, Sean, Nicky and then rhythm guitarist Flicker. Richey, unable to play any instrument, was delegated to van driver and equipment humper.

Projecting a debauched, tiny punk sound coupled with a cheap glamorous image, a cross somewhere between The New York Dolls and The Clash, the five put their plan into action; eyeliner, hair-spray and fake fur, mixed with leftist self-slogans on T-shirts and shell-suits. Then Richey had the good sense to come up with the wonderfully lyrical name, The Manic Street Preachers. Cue the music. Just about competent enough on their instruments, the four musicians set about writing their first tune in the cramped quarters of Sean and James' bedroom. Meanwhile, upstairs, Richey set about creating the band's political and literary manifesto.

As the pursuit for fan bases go, few bands world-wide could compete with the obsessive dedication shown by The Manic Street Preachers in collecting followers. Whether it be Goths, punks, glammed-up freaks, budding song smiths, graphic designers, political revolutionaries or the famous 'Cult of Richey' (drawn by Richey's sado-masochistic behaviour), there was something for everyone. The Manics covered so many bases that when they exploded on the scene it was hard to find a teenager who was not interested in at least one aspect of their presentation. This wasn't to say that everyone whose primary interests were politics, punk and literature would fall head over heels in love with the MSP. On the contrary, the young Manics made sure they stayed firmly on the fence. If you were a die-hard punk fan or intensely political, their interpretations usually fell quite flat.

But there were many out there who became interested in one small aspect of the band and soon became intrigued by the Manics' strange absorption of style, culture and politics. This was just what the Manics wanted. They didn't want heavy metal lunkheads or student book-worms; they wanted adventurous, open-minded culture freaks. In implementing this paradoxical method of attracting as many music fans as possible, only to weed out the ones they wanted, the fans gave the Manics quick cult-status. Manics fans were drawn together from the knowledge that they had broken the secret code and were in with the most happening band around.

"We are the Scum factor of the Mondays meets the guitar overload of Five Thirty/Ride while killing Birdland with politics." *Richey: 1989*

Teenagers weren't the only ones sensing a change in the cultural climate. The weekly music press, veteran vigilantes when it came to assessing current trends, had their eyes on the young Manics from the start. Change always brought new faces. Could The Manics become the new *NME* or *Maker* faces? They certainly had promise.

When the Manic Street Preachers released 'Suicide Alley', their self-financed début single in the summer of 1989, the music critics paid close attention. Sifting through the week's singles, *NME*'s Steven Wells came across The Manics' limited-edition (300) seven inch with the self-penned letter from the band attached to the sleeve. "We are the suicide of the Non-Generation," it read. "We are as far away from anything in the Eighties as possible, e.g. Eighties pop automation, the long running saga of the whimsical pop essay and the intrinsic musical sculptures of post-modernism."

"They have more anger and energy than any other band I have ever interviewed." STEVEN WELLS (NME)

Wells was intrigued enough by the letter to give the record a listen, and an ecstatic review: "White Rock Rebelboy single of the week!... This record positively fizzes with Clash Mk 1 juice".

It was urgent and frantic and contained all the trademark instrument tinniness and spiteful attitude typical of early Manics. 'Suicide Alley' stood out like a sore thumb compared with rest of the week's dreary dance releases.

Wells quickly arranged the first ever interview with The Manics, and a month later it appeared in *NME*'s 'On' section. Wells determined to première the Manics the way he found them. He was entranced by their physical energy, amused by their debauched rock'n'roll image, and bewildered by their political rhetoric. But most importantly he liked the game and was willing to play along. Employing no names to the sound-bites (even though the vast majority came from Richey), Wells created an anonymous mystique, riddled with outspoken political and cultural spite.

"They have more anger and energy than any other band I have ever interviewed," he began, and the band, knowing full well the importance of publicity, were well prepared to give Wells the show he wanted. "We are the scum that remind people of misery. When we jump on the stage it's not rock'n'roll cliché but the geometry of contempt.

"We don't display our wounds, we shove them in people's faces. We are the decaying flowers in the playground of the rich. We are young, beautiful scum pissed off with the world."

Richey ended the article with the sneering statement: "Wipe out aristocracy now, kill, kill, kill. Queen and country dumb flag scum. We are drowning in manufactured ego fucking. Boredom bred the thoughts of throwing bricks."

The interview was accompanied by a photo of Nicky, Sean, James and Richey kneeling on a London pavement, complete with DIY spray-painted T-shirts and printed manifesto in hand. By now, of course, Nicky, Sean and James had realised the importance of Richey and the potential he offered the band. Richey was by far the best looking of the bunch, easily the most intellectual and, most importantly, the most outwardly charismatic. Compared to Richey the rest of them seemed like Welsh simpletons. They needed a mouth-piece, and who better than Richey?

Flicker was dumped and James convinced Richey that he could teach him the rudiments of guitar. In exchange Richey could share all the lyric writing and interview duties with Nicky (who also benefited from a good jaw-line).

On the evidence of the *NME* piece, Richey could more than earn his keep.

'Revolution soon dies, sold out for a pay rise.' *'New Art Riot'*

Soon after the *NME* interview, the Manics released their 'New Art Riot' four-track EP, their first release on Damaged Goods. "'New Art Riot' was one of the first slogans we used to spray everywhere," explained Nicky. "It was our most grey, political and dogmatic time: we read *Marxism Today* and carried the Communist Manifesto everywhere, and we went through a naïve phase of putting Lenin and Che Guevara posters on our walls. But it was the height of Madchester – a barren time for lyrics – so we were determined to say something."

"'New Art Riot' was one of the first slogans we used to spray everywhere.'
NICKY

The cover, designed by Richey, depicted an EEC flag. "It was the EEC flag, but all fucked-up," he said. "The title was 'Collapsed European Stars'. The thinking there was that Europe was better than any form of nationalism, but we still don't necessarily agree with a federalist super-state. We think countries should develop at their own religious, political and historic levels.

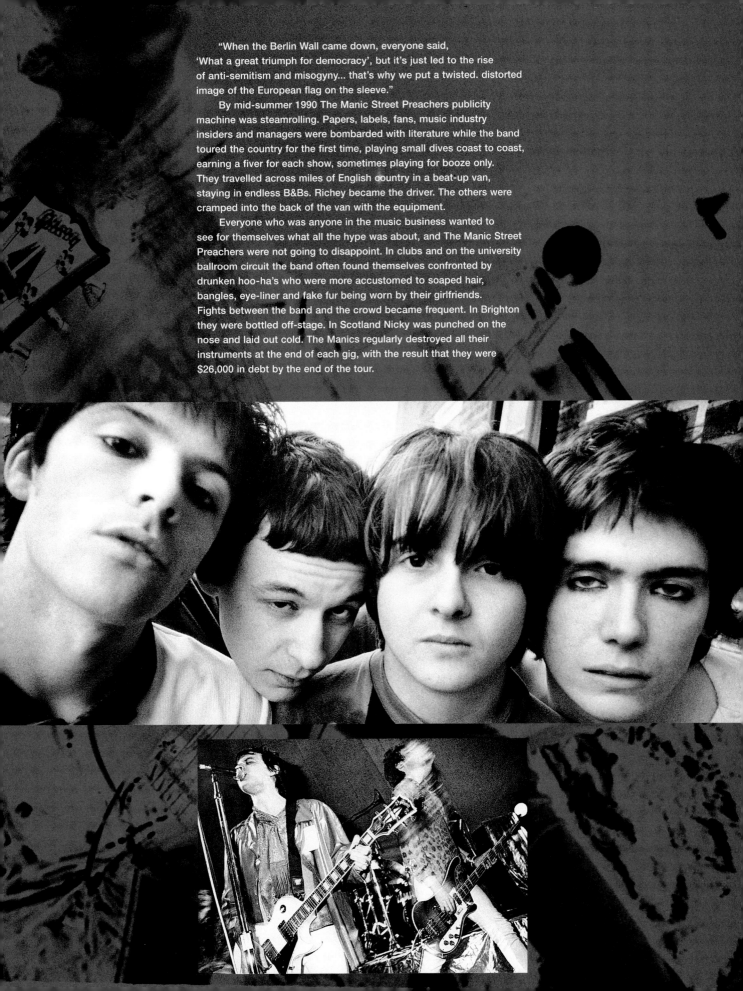

"When the Berlin Wall came down, everyone said, 'What a great triumph for democracy', but it's just led to the rise of anti-semitism and misogyny... that's why we put a twisted, distorted image of the European flag on the sleeve."

By mid-summer 1990 The Manic Street Preachers publicity machine was steamrolling. Papers, labels, fans, music industry insiders and managers were bombarded with literature while the band toured the country for the first time, playing small dives coast to coast, earning a fiver for each show, sometimes playing for booze only. They travelled across miles of English country in a beat-up van, staying in endless B&Bs. Richey became the driver. The others were cramped into the back of the van with the equipment.

Everyone who was anyone in the music business wanted to see for themselves what all the hype was about, and The Manic Street Preachers were not going to disappoint. In clubs and on the university ballroom circuit the band often found themselves confronted by drunken hoo-ha's who were more accustomed to soaped hair, bangles, eye-liner and fake fur being worn by their girlfriends. Fights between the band and the crowd became frequent. In Brighton they were bottled off-stage. In Scotland Nicky was punched on the nose and laid out cold. The Manics regularly destroyed all their instruments at the end of each gig, with the result that they were $26,000 in debt by the end of the tour.

Three

Returning to Wales buoyed up by the exhilaration of playing live even if they were managerless and in debt. The Manic Street Preachers waited for a reaction from London. The gigs had been chaotic, but nevertheless effective. Labels were pursuing them and they had captured the interest of the music magazines. More importantly, they had caught the eye of one Philip Hall, a PR guru and former employee of Stiff Records, who'd been entranced by a tape and the single photo that the Manics had sent him. Finally, after witnessing one of the Manics' fire-bomb gigs, he was converted. Hall felt that with a little work they had enormous potential to make it big.

Hall wrote to the Manics in Wales offering his managerial services. The Manics were overjoyed. Hall knew the first step was to get the band to London, and offered to let them stay with him and his wife Terri at their West London house. He also offered to fund them until a record deal was signed, a gesture that cost him £45,000. The Manics were stunned. They couldn't believe that someone besides themselves actually thought they could make it. They packed their belongings, bid farewell to Wales and headed for London.

"It makes your diaphragm vibrate and your appendages tremble." STUART BRAILIE (NME)

Maximising their exposure, Hall packed them off to any and all engagements, parties and interviews he could muster-up. Living together, Hall and the Manics soon became very close, with Hall showing almost fatherly concern for the boys. One early interview he arranged for the band took place outside Buckingham Palace, the scene of a notorious Sex Pistols signing. The Manics also revealed that their musical goal was to release one double-album before disbanding.

"Whether we sell millions and millions of albums, or we fail abjectly, we'll still have said everything we have to say in one double album," explained Nicky. "We don't want to look beyond that, because we'd just be treating it as a career. If you throw it away when you're the biggest band in the world, then you're bound to get respect."

But with only a handful of songs written, it would take more than idle boasts to silence those critics who believed they were little more than a flash in the pan. Many critics didn't believe they had the will, or the songs, to live up to their manifesto.

Nevertheless, the Manics set to work. Richey and Nicky delved into their note books selecting a snippet here and a snippet there, piecing them together and handing them over to an eager James who was feverishly working on a musical complement. "We just write our thoughts without any regard for structure or tune," explained Richey. "It's up to James to fit it in. Sometimes he has a really impossible line, or something he doesn't want to sing, so he cuts it.

We usually give him a page of words and let him choose. We've never cared about our lyrics being cut-up. Some of our favourite authors, like Burroughs, did that anyway. Kerouac never used full stops or commas."

By January 1991 Philip Hall had managed to secure a deal for The Manic Street Preachers with the new label Heavenly, and was eager for the boys to release something that would silence the now swelling ranks of disbelieving critics. The Manics had begun a campaign of sending anonymous, self-praising, culture-damning, journalist-hating letters to the music press. At first no one knew who was writing the letters, but after a few weeks the Manics were finally rumbled. To many critics of the band, it was just affirmation that they really were hype. Meanwhile, in their West London digs, The Manic Street Preachers opened a bottle of Jack Daniel's, laughed between themselves and planned their next move.

"All you slut heroes offer is a fear of the future."
'Motown Junk'

Reading, cutting out and preserving written criticism had become a religion to Richey and Nicky, especially Richey who would brood over every word obsessively. Well aware of the expectations, predictions and opinions proffered by the press, they knew their next release would be scrutinised closely. The question was, could they hold a tune, not just create a punk-noise racket?

Released on their new Heavenly label late in January, 'Motown Junk' landed like a bomb. Backed by the damning 'We (Are All) Her Majesty's Prisoners', Manic Mania finally erupted. *NME*'s Stuart Bailie, hearing the kick-start fury of guitars following an abrupt Public Enemy sample, awarded 'Motown Junk' the paper's coveted Single Of The Week. "This is the blamming and self-righteous, and the wildest record this week by several large universes," praised Bailie. "It makes your diaphragm vibrate and your appendages tremble."

"(It's) a hate song. 'Motown Junk' is just a blur of hatred, a constant tirade," Nicky would later say about the song. "Everything in our lives had been one long let-down"

'Motown Junk' was not only a great song, structurally superior to anything they had put together in the past, it was also emotionally articulate in a way that transcended rage and desperation. While many MSP songs sound angry, the Manics are at their best when they combine that with despair, fragility and horror. Like Nirvana, they seemed able to successfully add an extra dimension to their furious street preaching. The Manics sound was now developing along meatier, chunkier, metallic lines.

The band had been listening to new music, especially new American bands like rap stars Public Enemy and soon-to-be mega-huge Guns'N Roses. The band were awe-struck by Guns'N Roses' world-wide success, despite their use of lumbering hard rock; and were bewitched by Public Enemy's cross-cultural mass appeal despite the glaringly confrontational race verbals. These two bands were enormously influential on the Manics, who even went as far as to sample the renowned samplers Public Enemy on the 'Motown Junk' single and prospective taster for the up-coming double album. Most importantly however was the Manics' slow-drift towards a fatter, distinctively structured commercial sound, the idea obviously lifted from Guns'N Roses. The Manic Street Preachers were purposely distancing themselves from the London indie-scene, that they felt, for all its efforts at promoting self-stardom, ended up wallowing in perpetual self-defeat. Or at least that's the way the Manics saw it. Why, just because you are considered a small indie-band, should you write songs that fit into that criteria? The Manics agreed that the next tunes they wrote were going to be epics.

Four

"The journalist was trying to say we were manufactured
and just hero-worshipping past bands. We play rock'n'roll
and we live rock'n'roll. Rock'n'roll is our lives." *Richey: 1991*

"They look like someone doing The Clash in a school play."
Steve Hanley: The Fall 1991

They had the image, they had the sound bites, they had the
fans, and now they'd delivered the goods. Major labels were showing
serious interest in signing the Manics, yet criticism of the band
had begun to sky-rocket.

Competing bands, annoyed at the Manics' arrogant cockiness,
regularly voiced their opinions in the papers. Nevertheless, the Manics
continued their habit of writing confrontational letters: lines deriding
the London scene as nothing but "Funny T-shirts, stupid haircuts,
cider and songs about your ex" didn't further their cause as far as
popularity contests were concerned. But maybe this hatred was
a good thing. It actually made them look more rebellious; anything
the press chucked at them they tossed right bank in their faces.

In the summer of 1991, while the Manics continued their
small-scale but constant touring in the UK, they received some
encouraging news. Philip Hall, who had been trying to postpone
major-label interest until the right offer came along, had finally
received the biggest offer so far from Columbia/Sony. The band
still had an obligation to release one more single on Heavenly, but
that was a minor problem. After the signing with Sony, they would
all be seriously in the money.

"Other bands hit journalists and it's very macho.
They think it's good. I would rather cut myself, because I feel
I can justify that, whereas I can't justify hitting." *Richey*

Just when it seemed that everything was going right for the Manics,
things took a bizarre turn.

Backstage at the Norwich Art Centre, the band were getting
ready for the gig when *NME*'s Steve Lamacq, then a vehement Manic's
critic, arrived in their dressing-room to conduct an interview. Voicing
his long-standing belief that the Manics were managerial pre-packaged
bullshit and about as rock'n'roll as Bill Clinton, Lamacq eyed the band,
waiting for a response. "I know you don't like us," Richey is reported
to have said to Lamacq. "But we are for real. When I was a teenager
I never had a band who said anything about my life, that's why we're
doing this. Where we came from we had nothing."

Lamacq remained unimpressed. The battle of words
continued. Then Richey produced a razor blade. Standing directly
in front of Lamacq, the guitarist carefully and calmly carved 4-REAL in
large letters down his left arm. Stunned, Lamacq took two steps back,
covering his mouth with his hands. As Richey's blood began to flood
the dressing room floor, a shaken Lamacq ran out of the room to
the nearest phone. The gig was abruptly cancelled and an ashen
Richey was rushed by ambulance to Norwich General Hospital where
he received 17 stitches.

As news of the incident spread, Richey was asked
repeatedly to explain his strange behaviour. "I tried talking to Steve
for an hour to explain ourselves," he said. "He saw us as four
hero-worshipping kids trying to replicate our favourite bands.
There was no way I could change his mind. I didn't abuse him or
insult him. I just cut myself. To show that we are no gimmick, that we
are pissed off, that we're for real... at least now people might believe
we're not in this for personal entertainment. We aren't wallowing in
any musical nostalgia like the music papers' Clash/Dylan freaks.
We might sound like the last thirty years of rock'n'roll, but our lyrics
address the same issues as Public Enemy."

"I didn't abuse him or insult him. I just cut myself..." RICHEY

Asked if he felt a dick-head, Richey coolly replied: "No. I just feel like the rest of this country – banging my head against the fucking wall."

Lamacq remembers the incident vividly. "Richey said: 'You got a minute? Come backstage there's one last thing I'd like to say'. So I went backstage and I said: 'I don't think people will think that you are for real.' And he got a razor blade and wrote '4 REAL' on his arm while I'm just standing there watching him. We carried on talking for another three or four minutes and by that time he was dripping blood all over the carpet.

"Ever since the gig I've been thinking about the futility of cutting yourself to pieces to make a point. It's like a Sid Vicious throwback – the final nightmare of punk as culture shock. A stupid piece of spontaneity."

Inevitably, Richey had the last word. "We're completely happy that people despise us, but when you get a writer who should be in fanzines, saying that he doesn't believe we meant it and that we're just a manager's invention, then I got so pissed off that I had to do it. That guy couldn't conceive that people can be so frustrated and pissed off that they're prepared to hurt themselves."

Before long a photo of Richey by Ed Sirrs, cuts'n'all surfaced. Complete with haunted eyes, bloody towel and matter of fact smirk, the photo was, to say the least, very disturbing. Arguments for and against publishing the photo spread through the press like wildfire. Some thought he was a fool, others, including former *NME* writer James Brown, applauded. "We've got to print that," said Brown." It's rock'n'roll innit? I think more bands should do that sort of thing. It's artistic expression."

More rational observers were of the opinion that Richey's gesture was an indication of something far more serious than wanting to have a bit of laugh. For years self-mutilation has been accepted as a symptom of an underlying mental problem, and it was understandable that most newspapers and magazines were cautious about printing the gory photo, opting instead for a written account of the event.

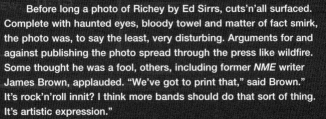

Nevertheless there can be no doubting that Richey truly believed in what he was doing. He was dying for the part. It was no game to Richey. While the others could submerge themselves in their instruments, Richey's priority was the band's manifesto. Acting as a sort of Minister of Information for the Manics, he took it on himself to project their image and message to the full. It was the one role in the band for which he was perfectly suited.

If the Manics still felt they had to convince someone of the reality of their mission, it certainly wasn't the fans. At the end of 1991 they were voted fifth new band in *NME*'s readers' poll, and their eagerly awaited double album was forecast as a possible highlight of 1992.

Five

"I'm a pimp, mate, I've got the wallet. He's the tart, he's got the legs." *Tim Bowen MD of Columbia: pointing to Nicky Wire*

"We signed for a quarter of a million in advance with £400,000 to make the album." *Nicky Wire*

On Monday May 21, 1991, The Manic Street Preachers finally signed with Columbia/Sony. Tim Bowen, MD of Columbia Records, had fended off competing labels who were encircling the Manics like hungry sharks. Bowen, strictly a suit and tie man and more used to Maria Carey than angry revolutionaries, stood out like a sore thumb in the signing shot next to the Manics.

"I signed the Manics, I suppose, because I went to see a gig in Guildford and thought they were the most exciting thing I'd seen since The Clash in 1977, who I also signed," he explained. "I just thought they were amazing; it's refreshing all the way through, even for an old fart like me."

With renewed vigour from the huge deal with Columbia, the Manics' confidence in interviews soared. The exposure was perfect fodder for the Manic Machine. This was the fuel the master-plan had always needed.

Heavenly Records were eager to get their last track out of the band, and the Manics, now working on a multitude of tracks for the forthcoming album, delivered one of their best. To the band it mattered little on what label the track would be released since it would also appear on the forthcoming Columbia album anyway. They handed over an early working version of 'You Love Us' which lacked the closing rock-out that had yet to be developed in the form that appeared on the 'Generation Terrorists' album. The band knew that a particularly rousing number was needed, a song that defined the new Manic sound, the swank, the pop sensibility and the usual Manic energy. 'You Love Us' encapsulated all of this. An undisguised two fingered salute to the legions of outspoken Manic critics, 'You Love Us' swaggers and struts with a blatant cockiness only the Manics could project. Who could possibly hate them now?

'You Still Love Us' was heavily guitar-driven, and very loud yet it retained strong pop-hooks, especially in the final chorus. It was their most animated single to date, perfectly showcasing the MSP style, sound and attitude. Reviewers went wild over it. *NME*'s review called the Manics the "most daring band in Britain", and went on to say: "It sends shivers down my spine just thinking of The Manic Street Preachers. Secretly, I'm sure, everyone wants to be in this band, living out their sordid rock'n'roll fantasies. They just won't admit it."

In a cruel twist of fate the Manics' best single to date sold only around 3,000 copies, not because of a lack of interest but because of a lack of availability. Even though Heavenly were hoping to ride on the back of the MSP/Columbia signing to sell records, not enough copies were pressed and little promotion was given.

The Manic Street Preachers' first single for Columbia was released on July 29. Culled from a number of songs they had been working on for the up-coming début album, 'Stay Beautiful' was a curious choice for a single. Sounding somewhat half-hearted by the Manics' usual standards, the song attracted poor reviews, much to the distress of their new label which sent word to the band to finish their début as quickly as possible.

Holed away at Black Barn Studio's in the small town of Ripley in Sussex the Manics were hard at work. Originally scheduled to take eight weeks, the sessions were now pushing towards their twenty-fourth week and still the album was unfinished. Columbia, upset by the lengthy wait and mounting cost, demanded a new single by the end of the year to compensate for the failure of the last, but even that was now looking doubtful. Inside the studio, the Manics were not exactly pushing themselves. They had a secure deal and money in their pockets, now all they had to do was make sure that the record was going to live up to everybody's expectations.

Steve Brown, noted for his work with Wham! and The Cult, was drafted in to make sense of the Manic sound. This seemed a strange choice but Brown brought the best of his production skills to the Ripley studio, reviving the slick pop production technique he had used with Wham! and combining it with the raw monster guitar sound he had dredged out of The Cult, to produce huge, loud pop-tastic tunes.

While James, Sean, Nicky and Brown worked and recorded the songs at Ripley, there was little for Richey to do but work on his rock'n'roll life-style. Sure, he went to the studio with the rest of the band, but he didn't play guitar well enough to add anything to James' advanced licks. Instead, Richey would lay on the control-room couch reading books, scribbling in his note-pads and downing vodka. Richey's musical ineptitude was never hidden from the press. On the contrary, the Manics always publicly championed the fact that Richey, the face of the band, had never bothered to learn more than a few basic guitar chords.

"Richey doesn't play on the records at all," said a proud Nicky during the recording of *Generation Terrorists*. "All Richey does is go to London, drives around, goes to Soho strip-joints, spends £300 on the Amex, comes back covered in love bites and asks how the track is going...

"We decided all that from the start. We (himself and Richey) can't write music but we can write lyrics and look pretty tarty. Richey's the spirit of the band."

The Manics' intention to record a huge debut album seemed to be materialising. They had a multitude of completed tracks, easily enough to fulfil the double-album requirement, and on the cusp of finishing their eagerly awaited opus they were still receiving plenty of media coverage, essential in making 'Generation Terrorists' the huge success the Manics had always boasted it would be.

"We (himself and Richey) can't write music but we can write lyrics and look pretty tarty." NICKY

It was make or breaktime for The Manic Street Preachers. The album's completion might have taken a little longer than Columbia would have wanted, but being their first album, the Manics, like any budding band, felt they were entitled to be a little over-meticulous. However, not a half a million pounds over-meticulous as some reports at the time would reveal. During the making of *Generation Terrorists* Columbia often found themselves at odds with their new acquisition. Many of the tracks had been worked and reworked many times over, sending studio costs skyrocketing, and the label had never for one moment expected a bill close to half a million pounds. When they found out, they made it abundantly clear to the band and press that they expected nothing less than a *Sgt Pepper's* from the Manics. To make matters worse, the band's recent bad behaviour at certain high-profile Columbia functions had added to their malcontent.

"Useless Generation."
Tattooed with a rose on Richey's left bicep

"The Manics address every subject with their own peculiar Preacher-patois." NICKY

Two months into 1992 and the monster that was *Generation Terrorists* is finally unleashed on the eagerly awaiting public. The cover, designed by Richey, was an everyday drawing of his arm bearing a tattoo of a rose with the inscription changed from 'Useless Generation' to 'Generation Terrorists'. It was the first whiff of an album that, from beginning to end, permeated the heavy stench of a wasted elegance not witnessed since Keith Richards during the days of *Exile On Main Street*.

The exterior look wasn't the only comparison *Generation Terrorists* would draw with *Exile*. In many ways *GT* even sounded akin to the classic Stones' album. This is not to say the Manics copied the sound, but rather managed to replicate the same tone of rock'n'roll decadence that had made *Exile* so infamous in its day. From the 'Rocks Off' kick-start of *GT*'s 'Slash and Burn', to the mournful pop lament of 'Motorcycle Emptiness', the stale stench of cigarette butts, spilt whiskey and leather prevails.

Bursting at the seams with a whopping 18 tracks, *Generation Terrorists* was everything the Manics had always promised it would be: angry and frustrated as punk, loud as metal, catchy as pop and as sleazy as a bad case of crabs. Owing much more this time around to Guns'N Roses than The Clash, the tinniness of past releases was now replaced with something altogether much meatier. Molten mammoth power-packed riffs combined with pure pop was the name of the game; indeed many Manics' fans considered *Generation Terrorists* to be their first pleasurable experience of heavy metal. It wasn't a heavy metal album though, despite Spinal Tappish song-titles like 'Methadone Pretty' and 'Crucifix Kiss'. As Simon Price eloquently raved, reviewing the album in *Melody Maker* at the beginning of February, "The Manics address every subject with their own peculiar *Preacher-patois* in which the words 'Culture', 'suicide', 'alienation', 'holocaust', 'slut', 'decadence' and 'rock'n' roll' are more common than the definite and indefinite articles combined."

To showcase *Generation Terrorists* the Manics released the album's best song, 'Motorcycle Emptiness', shorn down from six minutes to four. It was a blinding choice. A yearning, slow burning guitar ballad drenched with greasy despair 'Motorcycle Emptiness left the listener slack-jawed and simply stunned. "I don't want to go over the top," *NME*'s reviewer opined after naming it Single Of The Week, "so I'll just say that this is the most beautifully sad record since The Five Satins' 'In The Still Of The Night'... this is one of the songs whose luminescence will light our lives long into the future."

Nowadays considered an all-time British classic, typifying it's time-period, it's easy to understand why critics still hold 'Motorcycle Emptiness' it in such high esteem. It was also a hit with the punters. Backed by the all-time classic glam standard, 'Under My Wheels', the single had entered the Top 40 by March and was steadily heading up the charts; and this time around it wasn't just the die-hards who were buying the single.

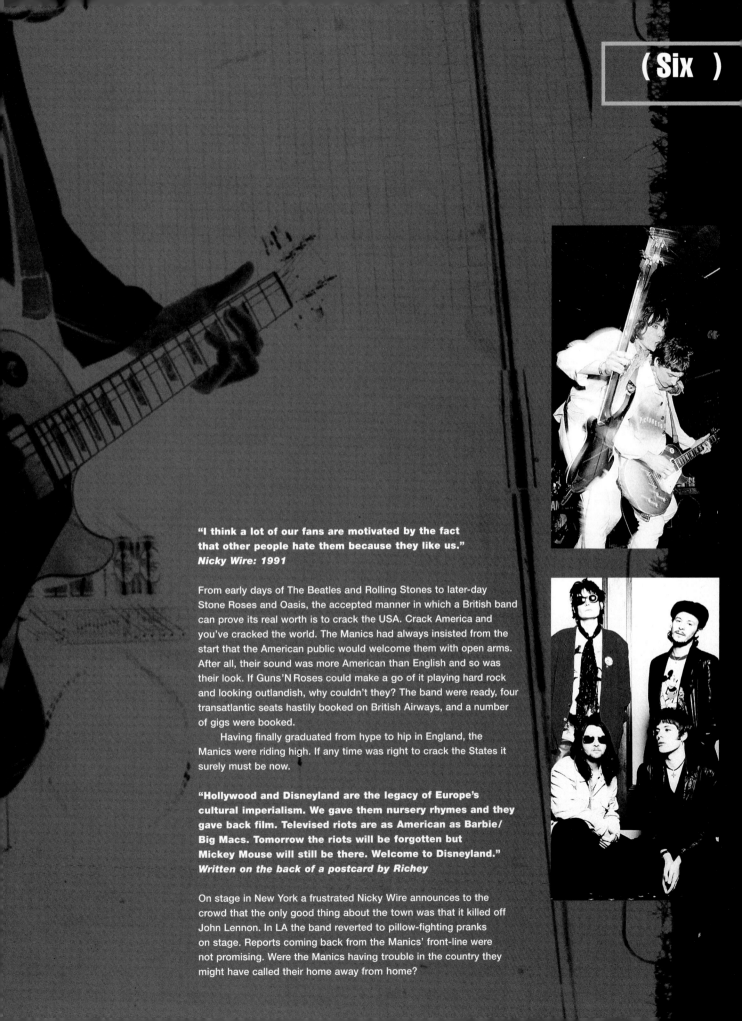

Six

**"I think a lot of our fans are motivated by the fact
that other people hate them because they like us."**
Nicky Wire: 1991

From early days of The Beatles and Rolling Stones to later-day
Stone Roses and Oasis, the accepted manner in which a British band
can prove its real worth is to crack the USA. Crack America and
you've cracked the world. The Manics had always insisted from the
start that the American public would welcome them with open arms.
After all, their sound was more American than English and so was
their look. If Guns'N Roses could make a go of it playing hard rock
and looking outlandish, why couldn't they? The band were ready, four
transatlantic seats hastily booked on British Airways, and a number
of gigs were booked.

Having finally graduated from hype to hip in England, the
Manics were riding high. If any time was right to crack the States it
surely must be now.

**"Hollywood and Disneyland are the legacy of Europe's
cultural imperialism. We gave them nursery rhymes and they
gave back film. Televised riots are as American as Barbie/
Big Macs. Tomorrow the riots will be forgotten but
Mickey Mouse will still be there. Welcome to Disneyland."**
Written on the back of a postcard by Richey

On stage in New York a frustrated Nicky Wire announces to the
crowd that the only good thing about the town was that it killed off
John Lennon. In LA the band reverted to pillow-fighting pranks
on stage. Reports coming back from the Manics' front-line were
not promising. Were the Manics having trouble in the country they
might have called their home away from home?

Fashion-wise the Manics and America were perfectly suited
for each other. They certainly looked like everyone else on Sunset
Strip or down Tribecka way and they acted the role perfectly: sleazy
clothes and gait, sunglasses bobbing while sipping Jack Daniel's
from a bottle. But while that movie-star image might wash on the
surface with the Americans, a more insidious and unglamorous sleaze
can often lie beneath their facades, especially in the creatures
that peruse the underbellies of New York or LA. In America's slums,
if you talk the talk, you have to walk the walk. It's no good looking
like sleaze-balls if you don't prove the point by behaving that way.

The band, especially Richey, had been fascinated and
lured by the American rock'n'roll life-style as promoted by bands like
Aerosmith, Nirvana and G'N R. Now it was in front of their faces.
Back home the Manics had always done their best to act the parts,
exaggerating in some areas, but always staying true to the game in
an English sort of way. If truth be told most of the band would rather
sup ale, watch cricket and get an early night than snort coke all
night with the 'babes'.

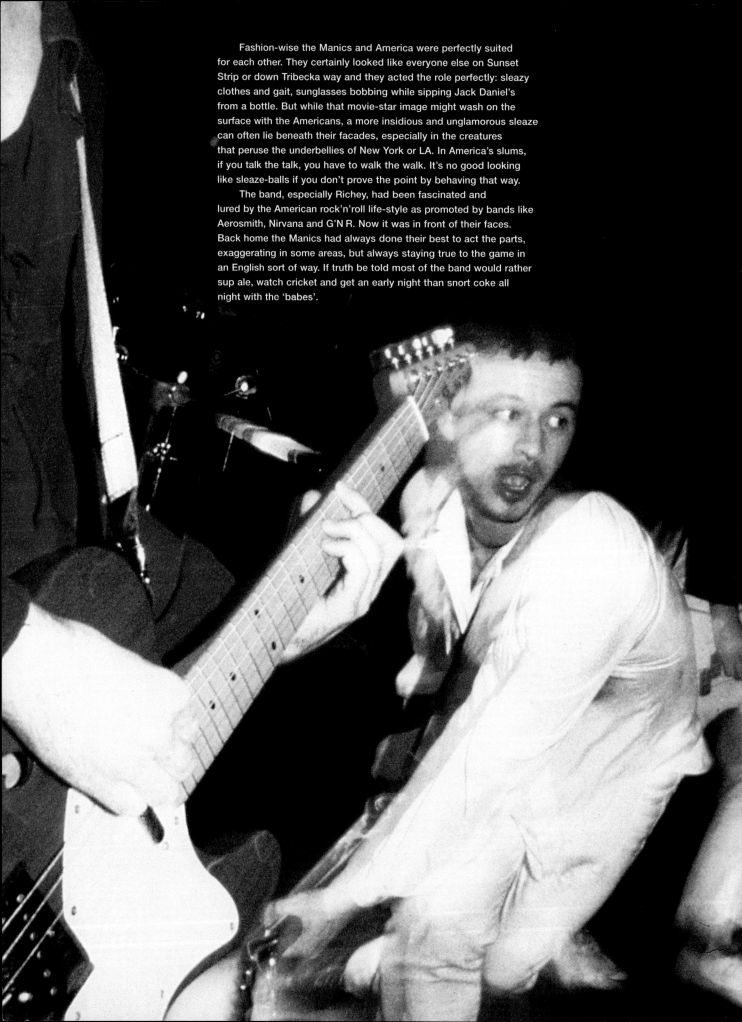

Like any other rock band they liked to indulge in nightly pleasures, but by the end of the week the band were worn down and bored by the endless groupies, drugs and booze that was being pushed down their throats. They were Welsh-boys. Maybe they weren't that suited to the States after all.

There has been speculation that this first trip to the States ignited Richey's long journey into self-destruction. The American cartoon take of rock stardom, the easy girls, the never-ending drugs and booze, had become too much even for him, normally the biggest partier. But while American overexposure to groupies and substances certainly offered that wanton-wasted fashion allure, Richey's abuse had always run much deeper than for fashion's sake. "Typical rock bands drink Jack Daniel's and get fucked-up because they have this romantic, glamorous Jack Karouac vision of the world," Richey would say on his return to England. "When I sit in my bedroom with a book and a bottle of vodka, I do it because I'm sad, not cause I think it's cool. I do it because I want to forget what I'm thinking about."

No matter what excuses or reasoning Richey came up with to explain away his abuse (being in a rock band is always a good one), there was no doubt that there was something more serious about the damage he was inflicting on himself. Richey's life-long obsession with American rock debauchery evaporated rapidly in the roadside motels he discovered from East coast to West.

"When I sit in my bedroom with a book and a bottle of vodka, I do it because I'm sad, not cause I think it's cool." RICHEY

Most of the shows were explosive. A taped intro of Allen Ginsberg was used to set the scene, then, when expectancy levels reached a peak, the band would take to a darkened stage. Not until the lights came on did they begin to play.

If the shows were the highlights of their day, the senseless promotion was often the low point. There weren't many Manics' fans in the States, so getting the word about was the primary concern. They were playing shit-dives to hard-core fans, those interested in English music, and while in LA it was easier because of the burgeoning glam-rock scene. Overall America looked a lot larger than it did on the map. Sometimes it felt that they had taken two steps back. Realising the band was getting increasingly homesick Philip Hall decided it was time to head homeward.

Returning back to the UK the Manics reflected on the moves they'd made throughout the past year. Having already claimed somewhat boldly that they would make 'the début double album of the decade' and then disband, they incredulously pronounced the future Manic invasion and conquest of the States.

While they'd been away, Columbia had been eager to release another single from *Generation Terrorists*, and 'Little Baby Nothing' was the overriding favourite. To these ears it was a bad choice; in fact, it was downright cheesy, easily one of the low points on the début.

The only redeeming feature of the song was that it included
ex-porn star Traci Lords (they had tried to get Kylie but she wanted
too much cash) on vocals. Perhaps Columbia felt 'Little Baby Nothing'
ran in the same vein as the anguished but far more accomplished
'Motorcycle Emptiness' and might even capture some new mainstream
fans. They were seriously wrong. The single didn't do well; indeed,
it showed how defective the Manics could be if they went too
over-the-top AOR.

Whatever the success of this single, *Generation Terrorists*
did prove to be a big commercial success in the UK. While it fell some
way short – to say the least – of the ludicrous 18 million world-wide
sales projection they had at first boasted, it was a better beginning
than most, even if they were sometimes loathe to admit it.
"*Generation Terrorists* is a fucked-up album because we tried so
hard to make some songs rock FM," Nicky would admit. "No band
in our position has ever tried to do that: write a six-minute epic
depressive song ('Motorcycle Emptiness'). I'd be easier and more
credible to make 10 versions of 'Motown Junk'."

What 'Generation Terrorists' did succeed in doing was projecting the Manics' package; their look, sound and attitude. They were no longer just another faceless band, but they were in danger of becoming over-exposed in their own country. Everyone in England seemed to know what to expect from the Manics before they even had time to make their next move – or so they thought. To survive as a band The Manics knew they would have to move away from the glammy image and adapt a new style and sound.

To this end, as 1992 was drawing to a close, The Manic Street Preachers accepted an invitation to contribute to the *NME*'s *Ruby Trax* compilation. *Ruby Trax* was a benefit album in aid of The Spastics Society and was not only a noble cause but also very high profile. Easily the most visual band on the benefit's roster, (which also included the likes of Suede and The Wonder Stuff, Kingmaker and Carter), the Manics, or at least Richey or Nicky, were almost guaranteed *NME*'s front cover if they agreed.

The Manics chose to cover the famous easy-listening hit 'Suicide Is Painless', the theme tune from the *M.A.S.H.* TV series whose gentle, breezy melody belies its depressing lyric. Almost effortlessly the Manics managed to transform the song into a full blown gloomy rock anthem. It was so good that it went straight into the Top 40 and gave them their next *Top Of The Pops* appearance.

When the *NME* staff heard the track their jaws hit the floor. Stunned by the complexity and depth of 'Painless', they voted unanimously to make it 'Single of the Week' and the Manics made the prestigious front cover, or at least Richey did: mascaraed, long-haired, naked from the waist-up and covered completely with dozens of small Warholish ink-prints of Marilyn Monroe.

''In the season of goodwill I hope Michael Stipe goes the same way as Freddie Mercury.'' *Nicky Wire to a shocked London crowd: December 1992*

Just as it seemed the Manics were set to end the year on a positive note with a smash single and high profile, calamity struck. But this was no natural disaster that couldn't have been prevented, this was man-made and readily preventable. This time it was going to take a lot more than an excellent single to redeem themselves with the press and public. Nicky Wire had always been inclined to making questionable off-the-cuff remarks on stage – as evidenced by the John Lennon episode in New York – but nothing could quite match his display of vocal vulgarity at the Manics' Christmas show at the Kilburn National Ballroom in London.

Around this time there was much media speculation on the state of Michael Stipe's health. Stipe was rake thin and some suggested he had AIDS, even though Peter Buck had publicly insisted all four members had recently been tested HIV-negative. When Wire made his remark the crowd – unsurprisingly – went mental. Fights broke out after the show and Wire was surrounded by an angry mob that included the Manics' support bands. They managed to make a quick exit but it soon dawned on them that Nicky had made a big mistake.

As word of the incident spread many bands and magazines publicly castigated the Manics, especially Wire. Even though they had always craved the spotlight, this certainly wasn't the kind of publicity they were looking for. Quite rightly, just about everyone in the industry thought it was an outrageously homophobic slur, and quite possibly a bad taste Manic publicity stunt that had gone drastically wrong.

It wasn't until months later that the real reason – albeit hardly a justification – for Nicky's diatribe would come to light. Philip Hall, the Manics' beloved manager and friend, had recently become very ill. Two years previous Hall been diagnosed as having cancer but had shown no signs of the sickness – until now. The Manics' knew it was now serious. While Micheal Stipe's illusory 'illness' was plastered all over the headlines, the Manics were actually having to deal with the real thing.

"I used to be really outgoing, but I'm more withdrawn now than I ever was." NICKY

"It's our fault if you make an album as good as it sells. If you don't it doesn't." *James: reflecting on 'Generation Terrorists'*

January 1993 saw the Manics scoop fifth favourite band and fifth best album in the *NME* readers' poll. It wasn't a bad start to the year, but it could have been better. Fortunately, the Manics were fully aware of the problems that had plagued them last year, and their awareness made the job of changing them all that easier. They knew they had to mature, both visually and musically.

Seven

The Manics were becoming too old to cavort around in
eye-liner and fake furs playing punky-boy rock and talking trash.
They felt they should go back to basics with the next album, to a
time when they listened to Big Flame and classic Led Zeppelin.
Not only was their fashion sense going to be replaced with a much
more stripped down feel, but their sound was too. James and Sean
had reflected for months on the musical vicissitudes of 'Generation
Terrorists', and Richey and Nicky had done the same with its lyrics.
They knew what had worked and what hadn't. This time round
the Manics wanted a whole album of songs in the same calibre as
'Motorcycle Emptiness'.

Eager as ever to prove their worth and knowing that a face
always seen is a face never forgotten, the Manics set to work on their
new album. They also moved out of London to where they felt most
comfortable, the West Country. For the album's production they
re-hired Dave Eringa who had produced their two Heavenly singles
'Motown Junk' and 'You Love Us'.

By the Manics' standards it was low profile time, but all
this changed when they were interviewed in the May issue of *Melody
Maker*. Nicky started the ball rolling with some worrying comments
on the mental state of the band, but in particular Richey and James'
penchant for drink. "I used to be really outgoing, but I'm more
withdrawn now than I ever was," he began. "I can almost honestly
say that I've seen Richey and James become confirmed alcoholics
over the last eighteen months. During that period there hasn't been
a single day where Richey hasn't had at least half a bottle of vodka.
Neither him or James can go to sleep at night without drinking
that much. It's pretty depressing. If they went out boasting about it,
it would be worse."

These revelations sounded pretty shocking but the band
had always had a reputation for drinking; apart from Nicky who had
cleaned up his act and become teetotal, which he thought gave him
the right to sneer. While James and Sean appeared to be packing
on the excess poundage (even though James was a fitness freak who
usually ran eight miles a day), Richey remained as skinny as a rake,
lantern-jawed, hollow cheeked and eternally gaunt. Vain as hell,
Richey was clearly on a liquids only regime which Nicky confirmed:
"Each morning Richey would wake up with a really bad hangover
after drinking a litre of vodka. Then he'd go to the gym, exercise,
swim, do lots of weights, have a jacket potato with all his grapes, and
then not eat anything for the rest of the day until he started drinking
again. He knew full well that in the rock'n'roll world it's either the food
or the booze in order to keep one's figure – not both. Anyhow, excess
booze and constant hangovers usually stave off the worst hunger.
It's true he looked good, he had cut his hair short, lost the puppy
fat and looked as rock'n'roll as hell, but again it was obvious that a
certain melancholia lay behind the eyes. Behind closed doors, and
remaining unpublished for the moment, Richey was still, in fact more
than ever, grappling with the inner demons that incessantly
plagued him. When asked to comment on the revelations in *MM*,
Richey was cagey.

"Yes, that's true," he responded to the allegation that he
drank at least half a bottle of vodka a day. "But it's only on the same
level as most people. Say if we were back home, working: everybody
I know would come home from work, go down to the pub drink
five or six pints, forget about everything and go to bed. I don't think
it's a big thing... I want to forget about things when it starts getting
dark. It's pretty impossible to sleep unless you've taken something;
otherwise you just lie in your bed and think about everything,
and it just goes on and on."

The *MM* interview also offered hints on the direction the new
album would take and there were also regrets over the last. "The first
album was more statement than intent," James would reflected on
the début. "This one is far more musical, more current. We were a

little too scared to make a hash of things last time. But we don't like slagging off past records. It's like we're despising our fans for buying them."

'From Despair To Where', the first single from the tentatively titled *Gold Against The Soul*, was a confident start, converting a rush of melancholia into a grandiose groove that would prove to be perfectly suited to big-rock arenas. If there was one aspect of The Manic Street Preachers that must always be commended it was their ability, even from the outset, not to sound like an inde-band. Even their earliest blueprints seemed deliberately crafted to suit larger venues.

By the end of March, *Gold Against The Soul* had been completed, and even though its release didn't inspire the same excitement and anticipation as *Generation Terrorists*, it was still big news. If the single was any indication of how the rest of the album was going to sound, the Manics could well be destined to stardom. If they had produced ten or a dozen songs of the same calibre as 'From Despair To Where', then they were a potential big-ticket.

In the event, *Gold Against The Soul* was good but not great. It didn't contain 10 'Motorcycle Emptiness" or 'Despairs' but it did display the band's new sense of maturity to good effect. The Marxist rants and the theatrical, boyish insecurities of the past were replaced with a harder, grittier and much more personal slant on life's everyday hardships.

Inevitably, the album's depressive lyrics came from Richey, and were obviously a personal reflection of his life. He wrote beautiful lyrics, but they were so damn depressing. The Manic Street Preachers greatest trick was in constructing up-lifting tunes that managed to incorporate Richey's dark undercurrents. Always as close as brothers, spending every waking minute together since childhood, they had forged a bond that enabled them to perfectly complement each other's talents. No-one knew Richey as well as the other three and while they only rarely spoke about his problems publicly, they could always relate to him through their music.

Many consider *Gold Against The Soul* as being no more than an up-dated version of *Generation Terrorists*, but it was much better produced, less raw and a lot more slicker. *Gold Against The Soul* succeeded in retaining the pop flavour of the début yet at the same time offered more lyrical and musical depth than its predecessor. The first three tracks make the point. From the opening bone-crunching musical stomp of 'Sleepflower' to the helplessly sad ruminations of 'La Tristesse Durera' (loosely translated from Van Gogh's final words as "the sadness goes on"), it's obvious the Manics were aiming higher. These songs sounded far more confident and direct than before, as if the Manics were finding themselves as a band. They had even managed to coerce Richey into the sound-booth to add some riffs of his own. "I've been getting better as a guitarist, and did actually play some guitar on this record," Richey explained. "But I don't know if that was just to amuse the other members."

The album spawned four singles, all of them achingly mature pop songs and tear jerkers, but the Manics hadn't gone all mushy. There were also raging power-chord riffers, harder edged tracks like the stunning and slamming 'Nostalgic Pushhead', and 'Sleepflower' whose lyrics dealt with Richey's inability to sleep without chemical help.

By the end of 1993 *Gold Against The Soul* had sold enough copies to go gold in England. Christmas was around the corner and they had begun the 'GATS' tour to promote the new release. The tickets had sold well; finally they felt they were appreciated for something other than the colour of their eye-liner. Then, just before the end of December celebrations, disaster struck again. Philip Hall finally lost his battle against cancer, dying at the age 34. Almost a brother to the Manics, he had believed in them when no one else did. His brother Martin took over the managerial duties but his death was a hard blow for the band, especially Richey.

"He had a big impact on our lives," admitted Richey. "He was the first person that ever believed in our music, the first to respond to all the stupidly long letters that we would send out to everybody we could think of. He said, 'I'll come to London'. We said we couldn't get a gig in London, So he drove to see us rehearse in a crappy school room.

"Before we had a record deal, he'd only recently been married, and he told us, 'You've got no money, you can live with us'. We stayed with him for a year in Shepherds Bush, sleeping in two spare-rooms, the kitchen and the lounge."

Hall would be sorely missed. It was to be another sad winter for The Manic Street Preachers.

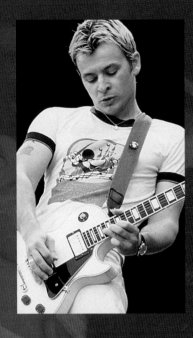

"I'm the sort of person who wakes up in the morning and needs to pour a bottle down my throat." RICHEY

Eight

Some thought it was the first short American tour, others the
death of Philip Hall. Some insisted he was like that from a child.
But whatever the casual agent that precipitated his illness, there was
no doubt that by 1994 Richey was on the brink. His drinking had
increased yet again, some say to a litre of vodka a day. He was also
smoking 40 cigarettes daily, and taking whatever drugs took his
immediate fancy. His self-mutilation and anorexia hadn't gotten better;
in fact, if anything, they had been getting worse.

"I'm the sort of person who wakes up in the morning and
needs to pour a bottle down my throat," Richey would tell the *MM* in
January. "I am paranoid about not being able to sleep. And if by
about eight o'clock at night I haven't had a drink I get massive panic
attacks and I'll be awake all night, and that's my biggest nightmare.
I can't stomach that thought. That's why I drink. It's a very simple
choice. I know that until one in the afternoon I'm going to be shaky
and have cold sweats. By six o'clock I feel good , but by eight it
starts coming around again, the thought of not sleeping. And that's
when I start drinking."

On their first full-scale world tour to promote *Gold Against
The Soul* the Manics had, at Richey's insistence, visited the Hiroshima
Monument in Japan, and the notorious concentration camp of
Dachau in Germany. Richey, who had studied Second World War Nazi
atrocities at college, felt strongly drawn to the macabre allure that
both sites gave off. These emotions would prove an important factor
in his own psyche and in his lyrics for the Manics' next album.
Even though we didn't know it at the time, the next album would
really be Richey's, a personal testament of his struggle with life and
a savage compliment to Nirvana's just released *In Utero*.

In May, a taster for the upcoming album was released, and it was a scorcher. I remember thinking if this double A-sided single 'Faster/PCP' was any indication of what the prospective album was going to sound like, we'd better build a trench and hide. Returning to their full blown punky roots once more for 'Faster', it was the sound of compressed frantic urgency.

'Faster' was the sound of pre-*Terrorists* Manics but with one difference, this time they actually pulled it off. Replacing the once tinny guitars with a monster multi-track sound and a thunderous rhythm section, the track is pure unhinged punk. 'PCP' was also punk, but retained some suggestion of the Manics' poppier sound. Strangely, the brasher of the two songs, 'Faster', was chosen over the more commercial 'PCP' to showcase the upcoming album. That week on *Top Of The Pops* the Manics previewed the fiery single to the nation, complete with James sporting a scary IRA style balaclava which provoked more complaints to the BBC than anything else aired that year.

From the assaultive sound and vibe of 'Faster' it was clear the Manics were transforming again, though it seemed strange that after so many conscious efforts to deliver pop-tunes, they were now delivering such obviously non-commercial material, especially as they were on the cusp of becoming very successful.

The answer was that as the band's psyche had changed over the last year, so had their sound. It wasn't just all down to Richey's increasingly maudlin behaviour, the whole band had become increasingly moody. Hall's death was a precipitating factor. Nicky agrees: "Things have been building up probably since, without being crass about it, Philip died. It was a lot deeper than we thought ourselves. We blocked it off and went straight on tour."

"In Thailand, definitely for Richey and me, something just snapped. It isn't that we weren't getting on. We went to Portugal and had a terrible time and then Richey's friend from university days hung himself and, from then on that summer, it got worse." *Nicky*

It was a hellish time for Richey. Death was all around him. Philip Hall was dead. He had just heard that his best friend at university had just hung himself. His dog 'Snoopy' had died. And to make the circle complete, Kurt Cobain, the one other songwriter he had really admired, had just shot himself.

He was also becoming, much to his own disgust, a sort of macabre cult figure. The Manics were starting to attract a whole new bunch of fans, fans who would wait back-stage with sharp sets of carving knives and anorexic war stories.

When the band played a couple of one-off gig's in Bangkok, a fan gave him a set of knives and coerced Richey to hack slices off his chest before the show. At first the fan wanted to cut herself in tandem with Richey. He refused, but cut himself up anyway, in private, before the show. These fans only made matters more disturbing for Richey. He loved Manic fans and had always waited patiently as one fan after another told him their life stories. He never ignored or turned anybody away, not even the macabre ones. It wasn't surprising that he didn't want to write or play any more pop tunes.

"Walk in the snow and not leave a footprint." '4st 7lb'

To say that Richey's new lyrics were disturbing would be an understatement. For this album he was baring his soul and it was downright terrifying to see what he had inside. The lyrics were so personal it was like looking in a mirror and seeing Richey's gaunt reflection staring back at you.

Reading the sombre tone of Richey's new lyrics, the band realised they would have to adopt a rawer sound. They weren't going to make another pop album with these lyrics. No-one minded though, because even though they weren't as depressive as Richey, no-one was in the mood for anything else. They also knew that keeping the band fresh could only be achieved by constantly evolving their sound. In any case, depressing music sold. Nirvana had made some of the most depressive, but best selling albums ever.

While *Gold Against The Soul* had been recorded in a state of the art recording studio, the Manics decided that they really were going to go back to basics for the recording of the new album, even going as far as to record the whole thing in a Cardiff demo-studio to get the required rawer sound. By July, three-quarters of the album, tentatively titled *The Holy Bible*, had been completed. It hadn't been a particularly hard record to record, since producing a rougher sound was relatively easy in the unsophisticated demo-studio but marrying the musical accompaniment to Richey's lyrics again proved difficult. But these problems were minor compared to other events.

The band have always maintained that Richey adopted a much more happy-go-lucky attitude during the recording of *The Holy Bible*. He had been more involved with this album, lyrically, musically and artistically, than with any of the other Manics' releases. Nicky thought he was exhibiting more enthusiasm and drive than he had ever seen.

"I see it as a state of mind," he said. "One we were all in. When we were recording it Richey wasn't suicidal or anything. He'd just bought a flat. He was still drinking and he'd come in about 12 o'clock, collapse and have a big snooze and say, 'Leave me alone, I've had a big drink' in a nice Welsh voice. Then he'd get up and do a bit of typing and we'd record for a bit, then go around Cardiff and have a shop. Him and James would go out at night for a drink. It was actually quite nice."

Whatever his state of mind, Richey had always been one to maintain very high work ethics. He always woke up early and put in a serious day, whether it would art-work, lyrics or interviews. Yes despite how Richey might have appeared to everyone on the surface he was now rapidly deteriorating within. Maybe, it was part of the curse the Manics had never been able to shake off. Maybe it was destiny.

Whatever the circumstances, Richey suffered a serious mental breakdown just before the release of *The Holy Bible* and, when it was released, disappeared for 48 hours. As a result, the record's revelatory lyrics were evaluated in an even more chilling context than ever before. Weeks later Nicky would reflect on really how *The Holy Bible* had affected Richey. "I wonder whether Richey felt he had to justify himself. The lyrics on *The Holy Bible* were so harrowing that a lot of the press would say 'How can you justify these records unless you top yourself afterwards?'"

In July it all came to a head. The band realised that Richey needed a little or a lot of space depending on how severe it was this time. At first they collectively thought, 'Yeah, we've seen it all before', but after many hours had past and there was still no sign of him the seriousness of the matter dawned heavily on them. They all felt for the first time that Richey might be in real trouble.

"The best thing is knowing that no-one can do fucking anything about it. People can't actually hold you down and force food into your mouth. And someone can't be near you 24 hours a day to stop you doing something to your body." *Richey after being taken to hospital*

When Richey did reappear he was horribly scarred from a two day spell of self-mutilation and alcohol abuse. His parents were so shocked by what they saw they immediately committed him to Whitchurch Hospital in Cardiff. Richey was given massive doses of

"I wonder whether Richey felt he had to justify himself..." NICKY

Librium and hospitalised alongside other similarly afflicted patients. At one stage during his stay at Whitchurch he asked the rest of the Manics if he could leave the band and only contribute lyrics and artwork, but he later changed his mind and retracted the offer. After eight days at Whitchurch Richey's family and friends moved him to Priory Hospital in South London which specialises in the treatment of depression, anorexia and alcoholism. On arrival Richey decided to accept the help on offer, and was immediately put on a 12-step programme.

The Holy Bible was released on August 30, 1994. It had little in common with the Manics' previous releases. The colour and flash that had made *Generation Terrorists* so exciting had all but disappeared, as had the elements of heavy metal that had so successfully bolstered the sometimes weaker tracks on *Gold Against The Soul* and *Generation Terrorists*. While the last two albums, indeed all the Manics' material for that matter, had traditionally contained strong overtones of anger, misery, blind-rage and depression, they had generally managed to retain an underlying sense of hope; the soaring notes seemed to imply that if you battle hard enough through your troubles, at the end you will find solace. *The Holy Bible*, however, was very different. It was the bleakest, darkest and most frightening of all their releases to date.

Many, including the band, refer to it as their Gothic album. They also refer to it as Richey's album. He had written the bulk of the lyrics, some detailing his very personal problems recent and past. His self-mutilation ('Faster), anorexia ('4st 7lbs') and mental-health ('Die In The Summertime') all featured prominently. Perfectly accompanied by James' and Seans' stark, resigned, almost skeletal musical compositions, the sound of the Manics now owed more to Joy Division than Guns'N Roses.

Recording the album in the demo-studio had been a wise decision, the lo-fi engineering and surroundings giving James' vocals and guitar a very compressed and muted tone which pushed Nicky's stabbing bass into the foreground. This only served to intensify the near explosive rage that exuded from James every word and note; always threatening to explode, but somehow just contained. Almost as if mimicking Richey's mental state, James had somehow managed to perfectly incorporate Richey's sinister and emotional words to his own style, thus forming a dark musical interpretation of what Richey was trying to say.

By December, Richey and the MSP's seemed back together. They toured a double-header with Suede, concluding with a ferocious gig at London's Astoria where they totalled all their equipment. No one knew it at the time but it would be Richey's last gig. Indeed, to all outward appearances, Richey looked to have made a good recovery. For the first time since the pressure of his finals at Cardiff University, Richey surprised those who knew him by eating a chocolate bar, a gesture that implied that he had got over his anorexia. Then he went even further, cutting out alcohol altogether.

"Richey's self-mutilation was very private." NICKY

In January the Manics were looking forward to their imminent US tour and were working on new material at Blue Stone Studios in Pembrokeshire.

The band and Richey had also decided to make a concerted effort to be open and honest with the press over his recent problems. "I think he just feels things so fucking intensely," Nicky would explain to *MM* in August. "He always had this vision of purity, or perfection, a kind of child-like vision, that became completely obliterated. A misprint on a lyric sheet, or whatever would just upset him so much, and he got to a stage where he just couldn't stop himself from doing anything."

To add to Richey's burden, the 'Cult Of Richey' was snowballing. Somewhat inevitably, the lyrical tone of *The Holy Bible* coupled with Richey's psychological afflictions added cryptic intrigue with the result that the cult increased by ten-fold. *NME* and *MM* began to receive an endless stream of letters from supposed hard-core Richey fans who supported, sympathised and even encouraged his acts of self-destruction. It was the last thing Richey needed to hear his recovery. Richey couldn't believe it. He wasn't proud of the fact that he had given in to his dark side, yet these fans *were* proud of him for that. For Richey the whole album had been cathartic, almost a form of therapy to combat the horror, not wallow in it. "Richey's self-mutilation was very private," said Nicky. "There was a working-class disgust. Cover it up and get on with it."

Even Richey described his breakdown in great depth and detail, recounting: "I wasn't coping very well, and I thought my body was probably stronger than it actually was. My mind was quite strong. I pushed my body further than it was meant to go."

Then he walked out of the Kensington hotel and disappeared forever.

From the start the Richey James case attracted mass attention. There was an appeal for information on *Crime Watch* which triggered a volley of questions. Did Richey thumb a lift from someone at Auste Service Station? Who was the last person to have seen Richey alive? Did Richey jump off the Severn Bridge? Alleged sightings began to materialise.

Two weeks later, on February 15, a car was reported abandoned at Auste Service Station. It was a Vauxhall Cavalier and it was registered to Richey James Edwards. The police found no clues in the car to help them unravel what had happened to Richey.

When the story of Richey's disappearance and the subsequent finding of his car reached the press, a local taxi driver, Anthony Hatherhall, contacted police, claiming to have picked up a passenger similar to Richey's description and driven him to Auste Service Station, the last stopping place before the Severn Bridge. His passenger had asked him to park at the service station and wait while he made a phone call. The man disappeared for a short while and then returned to thank and pay the driver. It was later discovered that there was no public telephone at Auste Service Station.

On February 20, David Cross contacted the police with details of a perhaps even more significant sighting. A MSP fan, Cross claimed to have spotted Richey Edwards standing next to a silver grey Vauxhall Astra outside a newsagents near Newport bus station. He admitted to not knowing Richey well but because they had a mutual friend, he decided to introduce himself. "I said to him, 'Hello Richey, I'm a friend of Lori's.' And he said, 'How is she?' How is she doing?' I said: 'She's doing fine.' He looked at me and said; 'I'll see you later'." David Cross insists that it was Richey Edwards that he saw.

Countless others have reported spotting Richey both at home and overseas, but none of them have impressed the Edwards family. Nevertheless, despite all the publicity, they refuse to get their hopes up and have dismissed the tabloid tales as ridiculous.

The police admit to having heard from many more witnesses in the case of Richey Edwards than in most other disappearances, doubtless because of his fame, but they admit to having very few clues. In the hotel room that Richey was staying in they found a packed suitcase and his prescription of Prozac. In addition, there was a note which said simply 'I Love You', and a number of books and films wrapped up as if intended for a birthday gift. There was also an unexplained photograph of a house, and many have speculated that this is a clue to his whereabouts, but no-one – including the band – can recognise it or suggest its location.

Detective Stephen Morley

Pressed for an opinion about Richey's whereabouts, the police believe that the huge amount of publicity surrounding the case would make a 'disappearance without trace' very difficult. Until Richey comes out of hiding or his body is found, the investigation, and the theories, will continue unabated.

The rest of the band were devastated by Richey's disappearance, but they firmly believed that he was alive somewhere. The trip to the US was abruptly cancelled, and all band activities were abandoned for the time being. Nicky and Sean returned to their homes in Wales and James spent time in London.

Richey's disappearance devastated fans, who sent letters by the bucket load to *NME* and *MM* sympathising with Richey's plight and problems. The manner of his disappearance was awkward and unfathomable for everyone, including the band. They had every right to be angry, principally because he didn't leave them a note. Whatever his motives or the reasons for his action, the band would have backed him; after all, it was his choice. They would just have liked to know what he was ultimately planning.

"I wished he'd left us some note saying, 'Boy's it's for the best. But I still love you'." NICKY

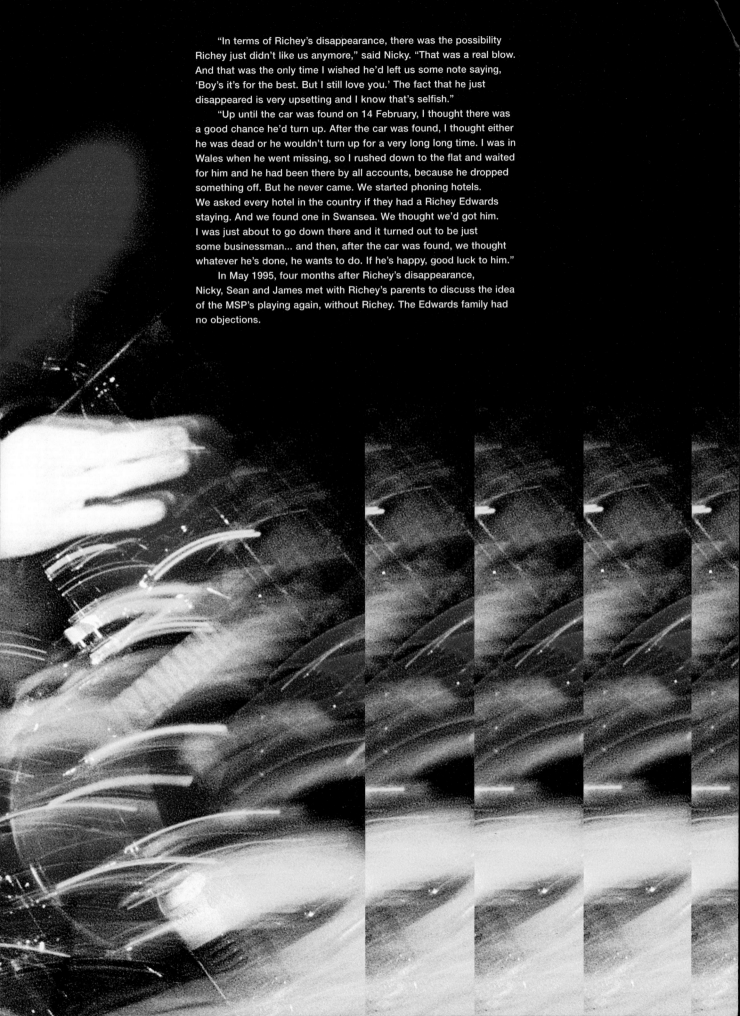

"In terms of Richey's disappearance, there was the possibility Richey just didn't like us anymore," said Nicky. "That was a real blow. And that was the only time I wished he'd left us some note saying, 'Boy's it's for the best. But I still love you.' The fact that he just disappeared is very upsetting and I know that's selfish."

"Up until the car was found on 14 February, I thought there was a good chance he'd turn up. After the car was found, I thought either he was dead or he wouldn't turn up for a very long long time. I was in Wales when he went missing, so I rushed down to the flat and waited for him and he had been there by all accounts, because he dropped something off. But he never came. We started phoning hotels. We asked every hotel in the country if they had a Richey Edwards staying. And we found one in Swansea. We thought we'd got him. I was just about to go down there and it turned out to be just some businessman... and then, after the car was found, we thought whatever he's done, he wants to do. If he's happy, good luck to him."

In May 1995, four months after Richey's disappearance, Nicky, Sean and James met with Richey's parents to discuss the idea of the MSP's playing again, without Richey. The Edwards family had no objections.

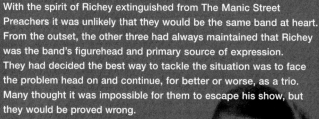

Nine

With the spirit of Richey extinguished from The Manic Street Preachers it was unlikely that they would be the same band at heart. From the outset, the other three had always maintained that Richey was the band's figurehead and primary source of expression. They had decided the best way to tackle the situation was to face the problem head on and continue, for better or worse, as a trio. Many thought it was impossible for them to escape his show, but they would be proved wrong.

Indeed, as they had almost always done throughout their career, the Manics would prove everyone wrong. Instead of curling up and dying at the prospect of not having Richey in the band, they did exactly the opposite. To survive they had to put Richey and the elements he had brought to the band to the back of their minds, and make a start afresh, almost as a new band. They had already been developing some new tunes in anticipation of going back to the studio but this time around Nicky took on the task of writing the lyrics.

Richey's final lyrics for the band were all contained in his prized note-book which was carefully bound and left in his hotel room. The band, especially Nicky, had read through every page and every word the note-book had to offer. As Nicky recalls, the revelations were blunt and painful. "Maybe one day we could use them and do an album of those manuscripts, but we need to come to terms with what's in there," he said. "There's some good stuff there... I know you can't get much bleaker than *The Holy Bible*... but after that we didn't think people were ready for songs about cutting the feet off ballerinas. There are no clues as to what was going to happen. Let's face it, you don't need any clues for Richey, ever since he carved 4-REAL on his arm, nothing would surprise you. Alcoholic, anorexic, drugs, self-mutilator... all your favourite things rolled into one."

From the extensive and generally morbid lyrics in his note-pad, five were deemed workable enough to be used. The band immediately threw themselves right back into rehearsing new material in the Cardiff demo studio they had used for *The Holy Bible*.

"It was just like the very first (album)," recalls Sean. "We were apprehensive and unsure of what would happen. It wasn't like we looked at each other and said, 'Hey it's still there... The magic!' It was just like normal. After 20 minutes we went shopping."

Aside from the lack of Richey's moral support, the band was still sounding very strong musically. This is not particularly unusual considering that even when he was in the studio Richey rarely practised or recorded with the rest of the band, but the real test of how they would cope without Richey's presence would be playing to a live audience.

"It's the one thing that's incomprehensible (playing live without Richey)," Nicky told *NME*. "Recording's not a problem. We are incredibly arrogant, we still think we are the best group in the world, we still think that we write the best songs. But without the visual, iconoclastic weight of Richey, as well as missing him, it's not right."

"We are incredibly arrogant,
we still think we are the best group
in the world." NICKEY

Ten

"If anything, Richey going missing has freed us a bit." NICKEY

"Every Manic's album has been a sort of reaction to the one before. *The Holy Bible*... I really enjoyed it, enjoyed how it confronts the audience. but that album confronts us, too. you play it on stage and you can feel Damien round the corner. It feels like handling a cursed chalice, you can feel the lesions breaking out all over your body. By comparison, *Everything Must Go* is quite comforting. There's a difference in Nick and Richey's lyrics. Richey could be quite nasty and classically nihilistic in that there was rage but no answers. And I loved them for that. But Nick's anger is translated into optimism." *James*

With a renewed sense of purpose, and new-found smart-casual fashion sense, the Manics set to work recording their first post-Richey album to be titled *Everything Must Go.* Set for release in July of 1996, the album was laid down at Chateau De La Rouge Motte Studios in France. Under the guidance of Mike Hedges the new album developed a lush orchestral feel, its tone one of resigned but sturdy optimism in the face of defeat. While fans may have expected a depressive backlash that reflected the year's events, it was even sounding strangely positive. "If anything , Richey going missing has freed us a bit," said Nicky. "We don't feel the need to justify ourselves because we've done enough of that. It's still melancholic, but we find that uplifting anyway."

In April 'A Design For Life', the new single and new sound of The Manic Street Preachers, was released, and it became the first Manic song to reach number one. It was 'an awesome pop song, perfectly capturing a tone of melancholy resignation within its stadium bluster. "A rock ballad of mammoth scale," wrote Taylor Parks in *MM* where it was 'Single Of The Week'. "Shadowed by massive and foreboding storm cloud strings, hinged on a recurring, lurching chord change that suggests only endless and unresolved anguish, it has, inevitably, a gravity beyond their intention, born from newsprint and speculation – but also an ominous, desolate momentum of its own."

The success of the single heightened anticipation for the album, but if anybody was looking for answers to Richey's final act inside 'Everything Must Go' they would be sorely disappointed. There were no answers, no theories and precious few references to Richey or his plight. Richey's lyrics stood out like sore thumbs, echoing his macabre style but the album most certainly did not dwell on the past.

Everything Must Go is far and away the most 'professional' of all the Manic releases. While previous albums all had their fair share of good songs, they lacked consistency. Now, for the first time, they had made an album wherein every song had the ability to stand on its own, separately from the rest of the album. Whether it was the slow ballads or the rock songs, James' multi-tracked guitar power chords dominate the proceedings. As the album unravels, the impression is that each song tries to outdo the last. The production is crisp, clear and very loud. There are great pop songs from start to finish: 'Design For Life', 'Everything Must Go' and 'Kevin Carter' all made an impact on the chart.

The three tracks with lyrics by Richey offer the album's only hint of bitterness, running along the same acrid lines as the mood of *The Holy Bible*. 'Kevin Carter', dealing with the suicide of the war-zone photographer of the same name, was a catchy little number incorporating some fancy Beatlesque brass whose musical tone belied the seriousness of the lyrics. His second offering, 'Removables', detailed his problems with self-mutilation and was framed with a rock-stomp track of which AC/DC would have been proud. Richey's third set of lyrics were married to the most disturbing song on the album, a quiet, slow and utterly depressive piece entitled 'Small Black Flowers That Grow In The Sky' which was more damning than anything on *The Holy Bible*. Amazingly, all three of these numbers, depressing as they were, managed to co-habit comfortably with their neighbours, sliding perfectly into the landscape. If anything Richey's efforts only heightened the new found optimism and poppiness than runs throughout the rest of the album.

Eleven

**"In terms of the 'S' word, that does not enter my mind.
And it never has done, in terms of an attempt. Because I am
stronger than that. I might be a weak person, but I can take
pain."** *Richey: October 1994*

So it's the end of 1996 and the Manics have finally grown up.
They've had to do it without their long-time friend and lyricist Richey
Edwards but nevertheless they've done it. They had just made their
best and most successful album to date and were last seen touring
the States with Oasis. Finally they were edging their way up the rungs
of the ladder towards serious success. In Britain they were more
respected by the press and music fans than any of their other musical
peers, Oasis included. Initially scorned by the media for their apparent
lack of '4-Realness' they were now the new darlings of the press,
respected for their personal and musical honesty and total lack
of pretentiousness.

And what of Richey? Is he dead? I doubt it. He had always
been fascinated with the art of disappearance (and towards the time
of his own disappearance was quite vocal over the possibilities on
how to do it). Nowadays it's not that hard to vanish into thin air with
the aid of a fake passport and a change of appearance. The faked
suicide theory is given credence by the fact that £200 a day was
being drawn out of an automatic cash machine by Richey every day
for seven days before his disappearance, as if he was planning to go
somewhere. Some say he disappeared to become eulogised forever
in rock'n'roll history; always in mind, never in sight. Some say he's
working in a factory up North with a big beard and a beer gut to
conceal his identity and that he wishes never to be found. Some hope
this is the case, isolation being the only deterrent he's found to keep
him from harming himself. Wherever he is and whatever he's doing,
I just wish him all the luck in the world and hope he's found what he
was looking for.